THE ADVENTU...
LEFT-HAND ISLAND

Book 4

The Upper Gulf Adventure

Godfrey Apap

This adventure seems lovely, perhaps it's a dream.

From West-East River, to Pointer Stream.

Story by: Godfrey Apap

Layout and Design: Godfrey Apap

Content Editor: Rebecca Apap

Stock art images: Adobe Stock

Illustration of 'hand map' by Sari Richter

ISBN 978-1-990133-00-8 (Paperback)

ISBN 978-1-990133-01-5 (eBook)

Cataloguing in Publication Data

Available from Library and Archives Canada

Note to reader:

These books are intended to be read to children

in those precious bonding years.

Then they will be read over and over again

when they can read for themselves.

TABLE OF CONTENTS

The Upper Gulf Adventure [South America]

~ Authors note ~

Book 4 is quite an adventure! The children meet some of the most fascinating animals normally found in South America. It starts off with plenty of songs and laughter, but at some point, the adventure ramps up. The children are warned to avoid the mysterious Pointer Stream. Concerned animals give the children some interesting clues about a monster. Of course, curiosity is a big part of being an explorer. What happens next is an exciting eruption of mythical creatures that you'll just have to read for yourself.

The Wonderful Wildlife

While inside the treehouse, Luc made breakfast in bed.

"Have some 'pan de queso,' it's a tasty cheese bread."

Then a lbig herd of llamas wandered by without warning.

And a baby llama said, "Buenos días - Good morning." [1]

Now llamas have long necks, much like a Camel-Giraffe.

They sang the Peru song, to make the children all laugh.

"We're Peruvian and we've got style.

Got shiny teeth and a big bright smile.

We eat corn chips, and lots of dip.

We've got some chip dip on our lips."

---

1 Llamas are the national animal of Bolivia. They will spit or stick out their tongue when annoyed. You can find them mostly in Peru, Chile, Bolivia and Argentina. A baby llama is called a cria.

As they began to explore, they saw monkeys in a tree. [2]

which sang the Five Senses song in complete harmony.

"Come sing along, ding-dong ding-dong, it's thaaah five senses song.

It won't be long, bing-bong bing-bong, you caaan all sing along.

You HEAR them make, the birthday cake, you HEAR the stirring tune.

You ask if you, can TASTE it now, you wanna lick the spoon.

You SMELL the cake, for goodness sake, you stay by oven-side.

You SEE the cake, it's freshly baked, your eyes are open wide.

You TOUCH the cake, it's your mistake, you made a pokey hole.

You TASTE a bite, it's yummy right, you lose all self-control."

----

2 The howler monkeys are one of the loudest animals and their sound can travel for up to 5 km or 3 miles of thick forest. The black howler monkey is the largest of the howlers and can weight up 10kg or 22 lbs.

On their journey north, Jacob saw something move slowly.

"It's drooping from a branch, like over-cooked ravioli."

"My name is Chew-Cheeky, and I love to relax.

I move somewhat slowly, like I'm just made of wax. [3]

I'll do what's important, that's to eat and to play.

But then every small move takes up most of my day.

Now I've heard of a bay, a most beautiful place.

You're heading towards it, at your current set pace.

The birds are so lovely, and the bay is quite grand.

You'll enjoy the beach side, with your toe-toes in sand."

---

3 Sloths are the slowest land mammals. When they are on the run, they can travel 2 meters in 1 minute. Their average speed is 0.24 km/h or 0.15 mph.

Then a monkey came closer, with something to say. [4]

It had something to do with the beautiful bay.

"Wanna sing a silly song – Do dah, do dah.

Everybody sing along – Oh do dah day.

Goin' to sing hoorah, goin' to sing hooray.

You'd better get goin' to see them birds,

Out by the big ol' bay.

Everybody loo lah long – Loo lah, loo lah.

Everybody bing bang bong – Oh boo bah bay.

Goin' to sing hoorah, goin' to sing hooray.

You'd better get goin' to see them birds,

Out by the big ol' bay."

4 The emperor tamarin monkey lives in Brazil. Both male and female monkeys have a white moustache.

By the Beautiful Bay

Deanna said, "Hey lookie, there's a bird way up there.

That's one of the biggest birds you'll see anywhere." 5

They arrived at the place overlooking the bay. 6

On the peak of a mountain, they heard this bird say.

"I'm Richar the condor, I'm up very high.

I spread out my wings, to soar in the sky.

I fly where I wish, I fly where I may.

I flew very far and got here today.

This part of the island, I find is so nice.

But listen to others, don't just take my advice."

---

5 The Andean condor is the national symbol of Bolivia, Chile, Colombia, Ecuador and Peru. Its wingspan is about 3 meters or 10 feet.

6 The bay looked like the harbour at Rio de Janeiro which is the largest bay and one of the seven natural wonders of the world.

Then by the bay they heard the splooshiest splash.

Kaitlin said, "This bird has a dashing moustache."

"I once lived in Chile, but I was taken to France. [7]

I escaped my small cage and arrived 'ere by chance.

Well zen bonjour and 'hello,' be alert and aware.

For zare's somzing not right by zah stream up zare.

Zis can be your new home, jus' get comfy and stay.

Jus' remain and relax and stay 'ere by zah bay.

It's so safe by zah bay, it's so pleasant and nice.

Au revoir and 'goodbye,' but please heed my advice."

_____

7 The Inca tern is an excellent diver and fisher. Inca terns are "piscivores" which means they eat fish. Both male and female are "monomorphic" because they look similar, and so both have the moustache.

Then they walked further north, by the lovely bay shore.

For if this was their home, they would need to explore.

Liam said, "Hey! A macaw with blue feathers that glow. [8]

With the shimmery-est shiny-est feathers I know."

"Hola, 'hello,' well now my name is Splay.

I sure love this place, what a beautiful bay.

I can fly here and there, I fly where the wind blows.

I'm as free as a bird, sort of free I suppose.

You must stay by the bay, things are not what they seem.

There's no danger right here, unlike up by the stream."

_____

8 The blue hyacinth macaw is 1 meter or over 3 feet long, which makes it the largest of parrots.

They continued along, when they saw a brilliant red.

A fluffy feather bump, on a fluffy feathered head.

Reese said, "Hello nice birdie, your red is so bright. [9]

So I'll call you Red Sockie, that sounds about right."

"Hello, my name's Doodle, wanna hear something new?

You're quite close to the stream with an amazing view.

You see this stream is lovely, it's a most stunning sight.

For there's a big waterfall, of the highest of heights.

Though I'd never been there, it's a sight to behold.

There's possibly danger, at least that's what I'm told."

9 The Andean cock-of-the-rock is the national bird of Peru. The male has the bright red plumage while the female has faded brown feathers. They are "dimorphic" because of their difference in appearance.

The Concerning Concerns

Jessica said, "Look at that bird, on a low-lying limb."

It was a toucan and his name was Tip-Toe-Tap-Tim. [10]

"Buenas tardes! 'Good afternoon!' It's a beautiful day.

Dis land is berry pleasant, so I sure hope you'll stay.

Howeber, if you decide dis place isn't por you.

Then jus' cross the stream with the remarkable view.

Now the stream is up north, jus' up from dis place.

You'll want to be careful, you know, jus' in case."

Well now Tip-Toe-Tap-Tim seemed so cool and composed.

But on the very next tree, a bird was highly opposed.

_____

10 The toco toucan is the biggest of toucans and grows up to 0.6 meters or 2 feet long. The bright orange beak is about one third of the bird's total length.

It was Tra-Lah the toucan who didn't agree. [11]

For she knew the stream was more dangerous, you see.

"Hold on, Tip-Toe-Tap-Tim, this much I have learned.

I went to that stream, but I should have just turned.

Whoever goes there will find a monster unknown.

You'd better think twice before you go there alone."

Well the children had surely made up their mind.

A home without monsters is what they must find.

Jacob said, "Should we explore, or should we all stay?

For it's certainly pretty, right here by the bay."

_____

11 The keel billed toucan is the national bird of Belize. These birds are playful, using their bills to throw fruit into each other's mouths. They can also throw fruit in the air while another toucan seizes it. Males and females look alike.

Well they picked up their courage so they could find out.

What all the warnings and monster fuss was about.

Deanna said, "Look there, that bird is about to speak.

He may give us a clue to the stream that we seek."

"I'm True Blue the toucan and I'm all filled with fear.

For the truth that you seek, may be oh so severe.

I've heard many rumours, scary stories and tales.

They've left me so anxious, that I'm biting my nails.

My feathers are falling and I'm molting like mad. [12]

If this monster is out there, then it's terribly bad."

_____

12 The yellow-ridged toucan has a yellow ridge on its beak. There are about 40 species of toucans in South America and as far up as southern Mexico. "Molting" in birds refers to when they shed old feathers to make way for new ones.

So they all moved with caution on their way to the stream.

They were biffled and baffled, was this monster a dream?

Reese said, "I see a small birdie, a colourful sight. [13]

He's so jittery and nervous, he's really uptight."

"Hello, greetings and good day. Pa-chew-chew is my name.

I heard a terrible sound, I'm not sure where it came.

It's an ugly strange noise, like a slippery slurp.

Or a bliffery-blurp, or a big-barfy-burp.

Just remember my words, for the stream has a stranger.

It's a place of much peril, full of dread and much danger."

13 The green headed tanager eats a mixture of fruits and insects. Contrary to what you may think, its flashy plumage is a good camouflage among the vegetation. Females have similar but faded colouration.

Then they saw a hummingbird, with colours so vast. [14]

He was flitting and flying, his heart beating fast.

"You're in the wrong spot and you're in the wrong place.

For soon you may see it out there face to face."

It's as mean as a pickle, it can give you a scare.

And the few that come back say it's like a green bear.

If the water boils bubbles and white steam appears.

Then the legend may be true after all of these years.

They say it has powers and it hides everywhere.

It could pounce anytime, anyhow, anywhere.

Go back! Go back! You must do as I say!

Go back! Last chance! Please do not delay!"

14 The fiery-throated hummingbird is found in Costa Rica and Panama. They are found in cloud forests at elevations of 1,400 meters or 4,600 feet and above.

Pointer Stream

There it was, Pointer Stream, with the remarkable view.

But the danger was something they didn't think through.

Julia said, "Look, there's the stream with the big waterfall.

And it's the tallest of falls, the tallest waterfall of all." [15]

And that's when they saw them, footprints in the mud.

Like steppies and stompies, but with a big thud.

Jacob asked, "Is this the bad stream? Should we all retreat?

'Cause I see heavy footprints from some pretty big feet."

Markie said, "There's burn marks by the edge of the stream.

Oh no! Now what? We're so close! I could scream!"

_____

15 Pointer stream looked like Angel Falls in Venezuela, which is the tallest waterfall in the world at 985 meters or 3,230 feet. It is so tall that the water turns to mist before reaching the bottom.

Luc said, "Zere's bubbles and round rippled waves all around.

And zis stream is now fizzing with a fizzy froth sound."

White steam started steaming, it was there out in front.

And this steam hovered low, bubbling out with a grunt.

Then up sprang an ogre, with rough leathery skin.

And it bounced up real quick with a splash and a spin.

It stood ten feet tall, like a three-meter wall.

It looked at the children and scowled at them all.

The ogre stepped forward, its big head came closer.

Acid drooled from its mouth, so it looked much grosser.

And with a low gruffly voice it said, "Do not trespass!

I'm the guardian of this stream, so no one shall pass!"

The children stood still, like feet stuck in a groove.

But their legs were braced for a quick countermove.

Their hope now seemed lost with this terrible stranger.

They had to think fast, for their lives were in danger.

"I can eat little children who come to my stream.

I can melt anything with my green acid cream."

Then it spewed from its mouth some green gooey ooze.

It melted some rocks and nearly sizzled their shoes.

Jasmine said, "Take cover, split up from one another!

The girls can go one way and the boys go the other!"

The ogre spewed down the middle with acid cream spray.

Luc was in the middle, but Jessica pushed him away.

The girls were on one side looking back at the boys.

And they all plugged their ears from the burfy-barf noise.

No one stepped in the middle, the acid would burn black.

Boys and girls were divided, so they couldn't turn back.

Then the ogre shot more acid in an arc to either side.

It made an acid floor cage that was thick and very wide.

Thus the ogre sprayed acid to surround them within.

They could now not escape the acid cage they were in.

Well, the children were trapped, they were dripping with fear.

It seemed their fate was sealed, and the end was now near.

"I will eat little children, for you cannot cross.

I will coat little children, in hot acid sauce.

I will rub my big belly, while I sing this song.

I'll make more acid jelly, it shouldn't take long.

Gruf-gruf! Grow-grow! More acid will flow.

Gruf-gruf! Grow-grow! There's no place to go.

Gruf-gruf! All done! My acid's begun.

Gruf-gruf! All done! Acid reflux is fun!"

Then out of the blue a bold bull-a-taurus landed.

This legendary bull saw the children were stranded.

"I'm Toro dear children. Ogre, leave them alone!

These children are harmless, they're not fully grown!"

The ogre grunted and roared and shot some more acid spray.

Bull-a-taurus spread his wings and the children were okay. [16]

As the wings repelled the acid, the ogre shook its fist.

Acid chunks fell into the stream, they sputtered and hissed.

The girls hid behind one wing, the other wing hid the boys.

Julia moaned, "All we can hear is that big barfy noise."

16 The bull-a-taurus was as big as a bull and had great powerful wings that could help it soar through the skies. Its fur and feathers were infused with perma-coated fireproof frosting.

Toro said, "I can protect you, with my wings spread apart.

But I soon will grow weary, you must all now depart!"

Kaitlin said, "Let's just swim, it's our only way out!

Wait, I see fur-ball rocks and they're floating about!"

Well five otters popped up and the girls ran toward them. [17]

The girls lay on their bellies, some tried to surfboard them.

Five more otters appeared, the boys slid on and cheered.

And they quickly swam away from the ogre they feared.

The ogre was dumfounded, it stood there like stone.

It was angry and grumpy, as it stood there alone.

17 The giant otters of South America are the longest members of the weasel family reaching up to 1.7 meters or 5 ½ feet long.

The children waved to Toro as they reached the other side.

And said, "Gracias! 'Thank you' otters, for a splendiferous ride!"

They saw a cute pixie fairy whose name was Butterfly.

And she gently fanned her wings to help the children fan dry.

Her wings made a soft breeze like the smell of fresh flowers.

It made the children feel sleepy, so they'd sleep many hours.

"The ogre can't swim from that side of the shore.

That ogre is just pouting, with a sour-puss roar.

You may set up and settle by the dimming daylight.

So buenas noches to all and to all a good night."

The End